TOKYO

NICOLA BARBER

WORLD ALMANAC® LIBRARY

54022582   1/07

Please visit our web site at: www.worldalmanaclibrary.com
For a free color catalog describing World Almanac® Library's list of high-quality books
and multimedia programs, call 1-800-848-2928 (USA) or 1-800-387-3178 (Canada).
World Almanac® Library's fax: (414) 332-3567.

Library of Congress Cataloging-in-Publication Data available upon request from publisher.
Fax (414) 336-0157 for the attention of the Publishing Records Department.

ISBN 0-8368-5033-5 (lib. bdg.)
ISBN 0-8368-5193-5 (softcover)

First published in 2004 by
World Almanac® Library
330 West Olive Street, Suite 100
Milwaukee, WI 53212 USA

Produced by Discovery Books
Editor: Kathryn Walker
Series designers: Laurie Shock, Keith Williams
Designer and page production: Keith Williams
Photo researcher: Rachel Tisdale
Maps and diagrams: Stefan Chabluk
World Almanac® Library editorial direction: Mark J. Sachner
World Almanac® Library editor: Jenette Donovan Guntly
World Almanac® Library art direction: Tammy Gruenewald
World Almanac® Library production: Jessica Morris

Photo credits: AKG-Images: cover and title page, pp. 8, 10, 35; Art Directors & Trip: pp. 4, 7, 11, 18, 23, 24, 25,
26, 32, 34; Corbis: pp. 21, 27, 41, 43; Corbis/Asian Art & Archaeology Inc: p. 29; Corbis: p. 12; Corbis/Bettmann:
p. 13; Corbis/B.S.P.I: p. 22; Eye-Ubiquitous: pp. 17, 19, 20, 36, 38, 40; James Davis Worldwide: pp. 31, 37, 42;
Panos Pictures/Stefan Boness: p. 39; Panos Pictures/Mark Henley: p. 14; Panos Pictures/Dean Chapman: p. 16;
Still Pictures/Jonathan Kaplan: p. 28

Cover caption: Tokyo by night glows with neon light.

Printed in the United States of America

1 2 3 4 5 6 7 8 9 08 07 06 05 04

Contents

Introduction

Once a humble fishing village, today's Tokyo is a great industrial and financial center and the capital city of Japan. It is also Japan's educational powerhouse, with over one hundred universities and colleges, world-famous art galleries, libraries, and museums. Tokyo is a popular tourist destination and the venue for many sporting events and international conferences.

◀ *Modern high-rise buildings dominate the Tokyo skyline. Little of old Tokyo survived the earthquake of 1923 and the bombing raids of World War II.*

"Tokyo throbs with a feeling that what is happening is happening here."

—Jonathan Rauch, journalist and author, *The Outnation*, 1992.

Tokyo has been the home of the Japanese government for over four hundred years. In 1868, it also became the center of imperial power when the Japanese royal family moved from the old royal city of Kyoto to Tokyo. Their splendid Imperial Palace remains one of the key landmarks in Tokyo, along with the beautiful gardens that surround it.

A City Reborn

Tokyo has experienced devastation several times during its history. It lies in an earthquake zone, and a massive tremor in 1923 left much of the city in ruins. During World War II, extensive bombing destroyed huge areas of the city. As a result, few original ancient buildings survived in Tokyo, and the Imperial Palace is just one of the many historic buildings that have been reconstructed. Many of the most striking buildings in Tokyo have been built since 1990. They include the huge twin towers of the new Metropolitan Government skyscraper in Tokyo's Shinjuku district and the amazing glass and steel Tokyo International Forum.

Life in this crowded city can be hectic. Many people who work in the center of Tokyo live in the distant suburbs and rely on

CITY FACTS

Tokyo
Capital of Japan

Founded: 1457

Area (City/23 Inner Wards): 238 square miles (616 square kilometers)

Area (Metropolitan): 844 square miles (2,186 sq km)

Population (City/23 Inner Wards): 8.13 million

Population (Metropolitan): 12.06 million (2000 Census)

Population Density: (City/23 inner wards) 34,160 people per square mile (13,198 people per sq km); (Metropolitan) 14,289 people per square mile (5,517 people per sq km)

Tokyo's extremely efficient public transportation system to get them to and from work. For some, this means a train ride of more than one hour.

Geography

Tokyo is situated on the east coast of Honshu, the largest of Japan's four main islands. To the east of the city lies Tokyo Bay, which joins the Pacific Ocean. Although the Imperial Palace lies on high ground near the center of the city, most of Tokyo is built on the lower, flatter land of the Kanto Plain. Historically, this gave

The Metropolis of Tokyo

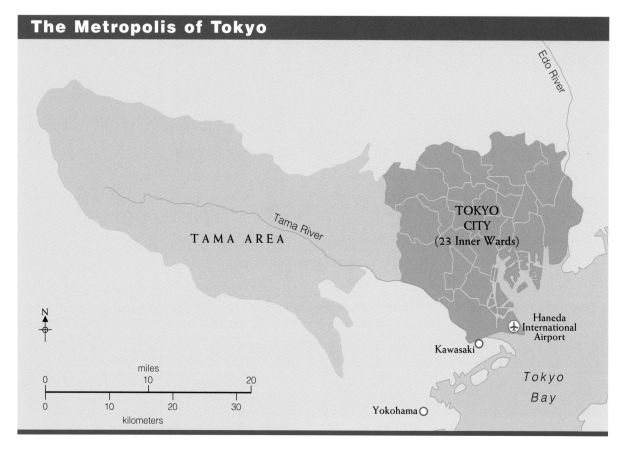

Tokyo City Center

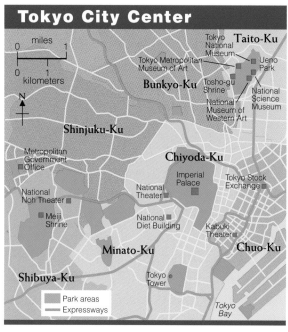

▲ *The Tama area and Tokyo city, which is defined as the 23 ku (wards) in old Tokyo, together form the Metropolis of Tokyo.*

Tokyo an advantage over many of the other cities in Japan. Much of Japan is mountainous, making it difficult to put up buildings or grow food. The Kanto Plain,

"Tokyo, Kawasaki, Yokohama, Hiratsuka all one great conurbation, stretching on and on to the smog-blurred horizon."

—Peter Tasker, financial expert, commentator, and author, *Inside Japan*, 1987.

however, provided ideal conditions for a rapidly expanding metropolis — fertile soil suitable for farming and flat land suitable for building.

Defining the City

The heart of metropolitan Tokyo is the city, bordered by the Edo River to the northeast and the Tama River to the south. It is home to over 8 million people. The city, together with the area to the west of it (known as the Tama) and the Izu and Ogasawara islands in the Pacific Ocean, forms the Metropolis of Tokyo. About 12 million people live in the Metropolis of Tokyo.

The vast urban sprawl continues far beyond the edge of the metropolis, however. A further 21 million people live in the cities and towns surrounding the metropolis and many commute within the region to work. With a total population of 33 million, this "Greater Tokyo" area accounts for more than one quarter of the total population of Japan.

City Districts

The city of Tokyo's downtown area is made up of a number of districts, each with its own character and associated with particular activities. In the middle is the business district of the Chiyoda ward; to the east is the "high town" area of the old city; to the west lies a new skyscraper district in Shinjuku; and to the south is a dramatic new waterfront built on land reclaimed from Tokyo Bay.

▲ The Sumida River runs through the eastern part of Tokyo and has its own public transportation system in the form of a water bus.

Climate

There are four distinct seasons in Tokyo. Winter is cold but usually dry. Spring is mild and a time to celebrate the flowering of the cherry blossoms. Summer is hot and humid with temperatures up to 86° Fahrenheit (30° Celsius). August through September is also the season for typhoons — fierce tropical storms that bring torrential rain. Fall is cool and crisp, a time when people love to admire the vivid colors of the leaves on the trees.

CHAPTER 1

History of Tokyo

Tokyo is built on the site of the ancient settlement of Edo, meaning "Gate of the Inlet." There is, however, evidence of human settlements in the area that date back to the Stone Age. In 1457, a warrior named Ota Dokan built a fortified castle in Edo, and today he is celebrated as Tokyo's original founder. At the time, Edo was little more than a few houses together with Ota's castle. In 1590, another warrior, Tokugawa Ieyasu, took possession of the area. In 1603, having defeated his opponents, Ieyasu became *shogun*, or military ruler of Japan. As shogun, Ieyasu ruled on behalf of the emperor, who lived shut away from the rest of the world in the ancient royal city of Kyoto. Attracted by Edo's safe harbor and by the rich farmland of the nearby Kanto Plain, Ieyasu decided in 1603 to make Edo the home of his government. Ieyasu's family, the Tokugawa dynasty of shoguns, remained in power until 1868.

Center of Power

Edo soon became the center of political life in Japan. The Tokugawa shoguns expanded Edo's castle and made it their headquarters. Five great highways were built to link Edo with distant provinces. They moved army

◄ *A nineteenth-century wood-block print showing life in the palace of the shogun. The kneeling man is taking part in the tea ceremony.*

and government officials to Edo and forced all the *daimyo*, the powerful landholding lords, to spend every other year in the city (a system known as *sankin kotai*). The daimyo therefore had to spend a lot of time traveling between their estates and Edo and maintain two households, leaving them with neither the time nor the money to stage rebellions against the government. They were also obliged to leave their wives and eldest sons in Edo when they returned to their domains — a further precaution against rebellion.

Under Tokugawa rule, Edo grew into a busy, prosperous city. Its wealth came from supplying the needs of the daimyo, the army, and the government officials who lived there, as well as from trade. By around 1750, Edo had over 1 million inhabitants.

Leisure Time

Edo also became famous as a home for writers and artists and for its leisure quarter, known as "the floating world" (now the Ningyocho and Asakusa districts of modern Tokyo). There, *samurai* (elite warriors), government officials, merchants, and other wealthy citizens relaxed by watching performances of song and dance called *kabuki* and a form of puppet theater known as *bunraku*. They also browsed in stores selling wood-block prints and books and visited inns, tea gardens, and bath houses.

"Revere the emperor: repel the barbarians."

—Japanese slogan of the 1860s.

The Meireki Fire

The layout of Edo reflected the social divisions in the city. Noble families lived on the high-level ground around the castle, called the Yamanote. The low-lying areas outside the castle walls, known as the Shitamachi, were where ordinary people had their homes. Conditions in the Shitamachi districts were extremely cramped, and fire was a constant hazard. In 1657, a catastrophic fire raged for three days, burning down the original castle and many other buildings. Possibly over 100,000 people were killed. Edo recovered from this disaster with amazing speed, however, and the city was rebuilt with improved fire protection including firebreaks — strips of land kept clear to prevent fire from spreading — and a well-organized fire brigade.

They might also have been entertained by *geisha* — beautiful women with exquisite manners who were trained in music, art, and elegant conversation.

Eastern Capital

From 1639 onward, the ruling Tokugawa shoguns kept Japan cut off from the rest of the world. They were afraid that European missionaries teaching the lessons of Christianity were a threat to their authority. The only Westerners allowed to enter the country were Dutch traders, and they were confined to a trading post on the tiny island of Dejima, near Nagasaki. Then, in 1853, the United States government sent a fleet of

warships to force Japan to open its ports to foreign traders. The arrival of the "hairy barbarians" — as the Japanese called Americans and Europeans — led to great changes throughout Japan.

▲ *This painting shows a fleet of United States (U.S.) ships under the command of Commodore Matthew Perry arriving in Japan in July 1853.*

The Start of the Meiji Period

The most important change was the overthrow of the Tokugawa shoguns in 1868. The arrival of foreigners on Japanese soil and the inability of the shogunate (the government of the shogun) to defend Japan's interests led to a group of politicians taking control of the government in the name of Emperor Meiji. They moved Meiji, who was fifteen years old at the time, and

his family from the old royal city of Kyoto to Edo. The city was renamed "Tokyo" (which means "Eastern Capital") and made the official center of government, law, and business for all Japan.

Rapid Modernization

Once settled in Tokyo, young Emperor Meiji and his ministers began a program of rapid modernization. They employed many Western experts to advise them and imported the latest scientific and

The Imperial Palace

The Imperial Palace (right) occupies the site of old Edo Castle, in the Yamanote district. The present palace buildings date from 1968. They are re-creations of the first Imperial Palace in Tokyo, which was completed in 1888. The palace was destroyed by bombs during World War II. Today's palace is surrounded by beautiful gardens in which the few remaining sections of old Edo Castle are carefully preserved. The public is allowed into the inner grounds of the palace on only two days of the year: on the Emperor's birthday (December 23) and for Ippan Sanga (the New Year's Congratulatory Visit on January 2). On Ippan Sanga, members of the royal family appear on the palace balcony seven times during the day to wave to the crowds. They are protected by bulletproof glass screens.

technological discoveries from Europe and the United States. Western styles in art, architecture, music, and even fashion became very popular. Many traditional Japanese styles, including blackened teeth for women and long hair worn in a topknot for men, were abandoned. In the 1880s, the Japanese government was modernized in the European style with a written constitution, a diet (parliament), and a prime minister. The emperor still remained head of state, however.

At the same time, Tokyo was booming. Many new factories were built along the Sumida River and Tokyo Bay. These new industries brought thousands of new workers into the city from rural areas and, by the end of the Meiji period in 1912, the population of Tokyo totaled over 2 million. Areas such as Ginza, southeast of the Imperial Palace, became very fashionable with the construction of new Western-style buildings. A network of new railroad lines linked the busy center of Tokyo to the outlying districts where most workers lived. The Tokyo railroad station, built in 1914 and modeled on Amsterdam's central station, was the biggest in Asia.

Destruction and Rebuilding

In 1923, disaster struck Tokyo. The Great Kanto Earthquake, and the fires that raged for several days after the earthquake, destroyed over half of all the houses in the city and killed more than 140,000 people. City leaders made grand plans for reconstruction, but these proved too expensive, and most of the rebuilding was haphazard and disorganized. Nevertheless, some major public projects were completed, including the first subway line

▲ *The Great Kanto Earthquake, which hit Tokyo in 1923, measured 7.9 on the Richter scale, but it was fire that destroyed most of the city buildings.*

(1927) and the first airport (1931). By 1941, when the huge new Port of Tokyo was opened, the city's population had risen to around 7 million.

The War and After

During World War II, Japan became part of the Axis powers, along with Germany and

Italy. They fought the Allies (the United States, Britain, France, China, the Soviet Union, and Australia). Tokyo was bombed 102 times by the Allies. Within four years, millions of people were killed, injured, or forced to flee, and large areas of the city were destroyed. By 1945, when the war ended, Tokyo's population had fallen to half its former size.

After the war, Tokyo was rebuilt once again. In 1949, the city was reorganized into twenty-three administrative units, known as *ku* (wards). The economy recovered rapidly, and by the 1960s, many businesses based in Tokyo were world leaders in producing consumer goods, such as televisions, refrigerators, and washing machines. Tokyo's rapid economic progress was briefly halted in the 1970s by a world crisis in oil supplies, but it quickly revived. Tokyo companies continued to export goods all around the world and invested heavily in electronics, robotics, and information technology.

By 1990, however, the city faced serious problems. The price of property, stocks, and shares had risen very fast, creating the so-called "bubble economy." In the early 1990s, the bubble burst. Many companies went bankrupt and thousands of workers lost their jobs. The city government faced a crisis as its income from taxes fell. These economic problems continue today, but Tokyo remains a dynamic, forward-looking city, with ambitious plans to recreate its former wealth and success.

The Olympic Games

In 1964, the Olympic Games (above) were held in Tokyo. This sporting event had great significance. It showed that, after World War II, the international community was prepared to accept Japan as a "civilized" nation once again. It also sparked a frenzy of construction in the city that continued throughout the 1960s. The Olympics brought thousands of competitors and spectators to Tokyo, which became the focus of media attention all around the world. Most visitors were very impressed by the city's fine new buildings, which included several beautiful sports arenas, and by the efficient way in which the Olympics were organized. For Tokyo — and all Japan — the games were a great success.

CHAPTER 2

People of Tokyo

Almost all of the citizens of Tokyo — over 99 percent — were born in Japan and have Japanese parents and grandparents. Most younger residents of Tokyo were born in the city itself. Many older inhabitants originally come from elsewhere in Japan. Many continue to maintain links with their hometown and make a ceremonial visit every year at the time of the *Obon* Festival, to pay their respects at their ancestors' graves.

Outsiders

Government policies have made it very difficult for foreigners to settle in Japan. There are about 200,000 people of Korean ancestry living in Tokyo. Many descended from Korean laborers who were forced to move to Japan to work during the time when Japan occupied Korea (1910–1945). Relations between the Japanese and Koreans are not always easy. The Koreans resent the harsh treatment their homeland received, while the Japanese do not respect Korean culture as highly as their own.

Konketsu are people of mixed ancestry. Many of them descended from Japanese women and U.S. servicemen stationed in Japan after World War II. They are often discriminated against because of their

◀ *Crowds of people fill the streets of the lively Shinjuku shopping district.*

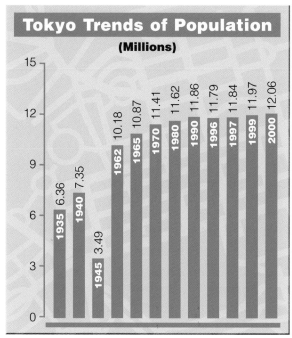

Tokyo Trends of Population
(Millions)

Year	Population
1935	6.36
1940	7.35
1945	3.49
1962	10.18
1965	10.87
1970	11.41
1980	11.62
1990	11.86
1996	11.79
1997	11.84
1999	11.97
2000	12.06

Source: Statistic Division, Bureau of General Affairs, Tokyo Metropolitan Government & Statistics Bureau, Ministry of Public Management, Home Affairs, Posts and Telecommunications, Japan.

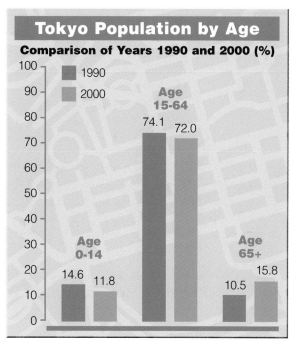

Tokyo Population by Age
Comparison of Years 1990 and 2000 (%)

Age group	1990	2000
Age 0-14	14.6	11.8
Age 15-64	74.1	72.0
Age 65+	10.5	15.8

Source: Statistic Division, Bureau of General Affairs, Tokyo Metropolitan Government & Statistics Bureau, Ministry of Public Management, Home Affairs, Posts and Telecommunications, Japan.

non-Japanese appearance. The majority live in Tokyo and work in the fashion or entertainment industries, where their looks give them an exotic appeal. This can be profitable, but many konketsu would prefer equal treatment and a wider choice of career. Although illegal, discrimination is also common against another group of Japanese people in Tokyo — the *burakumin*. In the past, the ancestors of the burakumin did jobs that were important but "unclean," such as slaughtering animals for food. Some Japanese people still refuse to employ them or let their children marry them. Although they look no different, people can identify burakumin by running illegal checks on their ancestry.

Tokyo Characteristics

Traditionally, Japanese people thought that the inhabitants of different regions had different characteristics. The citizens of Tokyo were said to be strong and to value glory and honor more than money. In practice, few Tokyo people conform to these old stereotypes, but they are still sometimes talked about today.

Tokyo's Foreign Community

About 300,000 people form Tokyo's expatriate (foreign) community. It is made up of businesspeople; teachers working in English language schools; and people working as cooks, nannies, and maids. There are also a few thousand *nisei* — foreign-born men and women of Japanese ancestry who have returned to their ancestral home to live and work.

▲ *A vendor sells food on the grounds of a shrine. Mobile stalls selling snack foods and beverages are often found around Tokyo's parks and stations.*

Unique Cuisine

Food is a very important part of Japanese culture, and Tokyo has many superstores, craft shops, and open-air markets selling food of all kinds. Japanese foods are different from those anywhere else on Earth. Meals are based on sticky rice, soy beans, and seafood, which might mean anything from salmon or shark to sea-slug and seaweed. Japanese people eat little meat and almost no dairy products (milk or yogurt). Instead, they prefer noodles made from the seeds of buckwheat (a plant somewhat like rhubarb), and many different fruits and vegetables, including white pears, persimmons, lotus root, and giant radishes.

Beautiful Presentation

Japan has little good farming land and, for centuries, food was scarce and meals were very frugal. Even today, Japanese diners still prize the freshness, taste, and appearance of

Sushi Bars

Some restaurants and bars serve nothing but sushi — tasty morsels of fish and vegetables served on little mounds of cold, vinegared rice, to be eaten with soy sauce and wasabi *(green horseradish). The most popular ingredients include shrimp, salmon, tuna, plums, cucumbers, pickled ginger, and octopus. Sushi is always beautifully arranged and displayed. Diners choose the items they would like — sometimes from a moving conveyor belt that carries plates of sushi past their table.*

their food more than portion size. Food is often cut into small pieces, ready for diners to eat with chopsticks, and beautifully arranged on plates. It might also be decorated with real flowers or tiny strips of vegetables shaped to look like petals and leaves. In recent years, this traditional concern with how food looks has led Japanese farmers to use too many chemicals, especially pesticides, to help improve the appearance of their produce.

Traditional and Modern

Throughout Japan, families like to eat together at home, but in big cities such as Tokyo, groups of friends and business colleagues often visit restaurants for a meal, especially in the evenings after work. Most restaurants serve traditional Japanese foods. Favorite dishes include *sashimi*, thinly-sliced raw fish; *sukiyaki*, little pieces of beef cooked

▼ This bento *(lunchbox) contains a beautifully presented meal of sushi — and the chopsticks to eat it with.*

in sugar and soy sauce then dipped in raw egg; *teppenyaki*, meat or fish cooked on a griddle; or *tempura*, seafood or vegetables fried in batter. For a special treat, diners might try eel or puffer fish — which is poisonous unless prepared by an expert cook. The traditional Japanese drink is green tea, served without milk, but today Japanese people also like fruit juices, soda, coffee, beer, and stronger alcoholic beverages, such as *sake* (rice spirits) and whiskey.

There are also many U.S.-style burger joints and fast-food restaurants in Tokyo. Japanese people usually visit these at lunchtime or when out shopping on the weekends, for a quick snack. Alternatively, they might buy a traditional *bento* (lunchbox) containing cold rice, vegetables, a little meat or fish, pickles, and a slice of fruit.

Religion

Japan's two major religions are Shintoism and Buddhism, but there are also small groups of Christians, Confucians, and Muslims. Religious minority groups have their own places of worship in Tokyo. These include Catholic and Protestant churches and two central mosques.

Shinto

Shinto, which means "the way of the gods," is Japan's ancient, traditional religion. Worshipers honor *kami* (spirits) in all living things and in nonliving objects such as mountains and streams. For most Japanese

▲ *The Senso-ji temple in Asakusa became a center of worship during the seventh century. The temple that stands today was rebuilt after World War II.*

people, Shintoism is a way of life. They visit Shinto shrines to say prayers and make offerings. They also buy good-luck charms and leave *ema*, lists of hopes and wishes for the future.

There are many Shinto shrines in Tokyo, including Hie Jinja (Mountain God Shrine) on the grounds of Edo Castle. Its kami was believed to guard the city. The Asakusa Jinja shrine honors the spirits of three Edo fishermen who found a holy statue in their nets, and it is the focus of the *Sanja* Festival (Tokyo's biggest), every year in May. Crowds dressed in traditional Japanese clothes carry huge portable shrines called *mikoshi* through the streets to the shrine to receive a blessing.

Buddhism

There is a Japanese saying about religion: "Shinto is for when you're born; Buddhism is for when you die." While many Japanese people use Shinto rituals to help them with everyday life, Buddhism in Japan is often associated with questions of life after death. Buddhism was introduced to Japan

Tea Ceremony

Chanoyu, or the tea ceremony (below), is uniquely Japanese. It has its origins in the thirteenth century when Buddhist monks drank tea to remain alert while performing their religious duties. The elaborate ritual of the ceremony dates from the sixteenth century, however, and has remained unchanged since that time. The tea ceremony takes place in a simple teahouse, with the host and guests on either side of a brazier (a metal vessel containing hot coals). They kneel on tatami mats — mats made from straw and covered with a smooth layer of marsh grass called rush. The making and drinking of the tea is all part of the ritual and follows a formal pattern.

"Even a common man by obtaining knowledge becomes a Buddha."

—Japanese Buddhist proverb.

in about A.D. 550. It originated in India, where a religious teacher known as "the Buddha" ("the enlightened one") taught his followers to seek peace and an end to suffering by following a pure, simple life. Over the centuries, Japanese people built many statues and temples to honor the Buddha and to remind themselves of his message. In Tokyo, the most important includes Senso-ji, a shrine that houses a statue of the Buddhist goddess of mercy. Worshipers go there to pray, burn incense, and leave offerings of flowers and sake.

Festivals

Festivals, or *matsuri*, are an important part of Japanese religious and cultural life. Some are very ancient; others combine the old with the modern. Some are nationwide and some local, based on individual temples or shrines. Matsuri originally came from Shinto traditions and were held by farming communities to mark important times of the year, such as planting and harvesting. Offerings were made to the spirits. Today, festivals take place in both Shinto shrines and Buddhist temples.

Many matsuri follow a similar pattern. The shrine is purified with water or fire, and then offerings are made to the kami.

The kami is then believed to leave the shrine to be taken in a *mikoshi*, or portable shrine, often in a spectacular procession that weaves through the streets around the shrine. There is often some entertainment, such as dancing or displays of archery, before the kami is taken back to the shrine.

▲ *A huge mikoshi, or portable shrine, is carried in a procession through the streets of Tokyo.*

Tokyo's Celebrations

It is said that there is a festival going on someplace in Tokyo every day of the year. One of the most important festivals falls on

Major Festivals (Public Holidays)

- Ganjitsu, *New Year's Day, January 1*
- Seijin no Hi, *Coming of Age Day, second Monday in January*
- Kenkoku Kinen no Hi, *National Foundation Day, February 11*
- Shumbun no Hi, *Vernal Equinox Day, March 21*
- Midori no Hi, *Greenery Day, April 29*
- Kempo Kinenbi, *Constitution Day, May 3*
- Kodomo no Hi, *Children's Day, May 5*

- Umi no Hi, *Maritime Day, July 20*
- Keiro no Hi, *Respect for the Aged Day, September 15*
- Shubun no Hi, *Autumn Equinox Day, September 23*
- Taiiku no Hi, *Health Sports Day, second Monday in October*
- Bunka no Hi, *Culture Day, November 3*
- Kinro Kansha no Hi, *Labor Thanksgiving Day, November 23*
- Tenno Tanjobi, *Emperor's Birthday, December 23*

New Year's (December 31/January 1) when temple bells are struck 108 times at midnight — a Buddhist tradition to dispel the 108 earthly desires that afflict us all. Everyone visits shrines and temples on New Year's Day to pray for luck in the year ahead and to buy lucky charms.

Many festivals are specific to Tokyo. The "big three" festivals in the city are the *Kanda*, *Sanja*, and *Sanno* festivals, which are held in May and June with many portable shrines and lots of entertainment. On January 6, *Dezome-shiki* takes place on the plaza in front of the Tokyo International Exhibition Center, a huge conference center better known as "Tokyo Big Sight." This is a spectacular parade put on by the city's fire

Beautiful Blossoms

Hanami, or blossom viewing, is a major festival across Japan. It is held in springtime, in late March and early April, as the cherry blossoms (above) come into flower. These blossoms last only a week or so, and people hold parties beneath the trees, with lunch boxes and sake. Popular places to hold hanami parties in Tokyo include Ueno Park, Sumida Park, Yasukuni Shrine, and Aoyama Cemetery.

department, culminating in an acrobatic display by firefighters dressed in Edo-era costumes. In late September, moon-viewing parties are a tradition. They date back to the Edo period of Tokyo.

CHAPTER 3

Living in Tokyo

The rapid increase of the population of Tokyo has led to a serious shortage of housing in the city. Even if people can find accommodations, most probably cannot afford to pay for them — the price of land soared during the late 1980s, inflating the cost of houses and apartments. Most people live in the relatively cheap outlying districts of Tokyo and spend at least two hours every day commuting to work. Compared with the rest of Japan, the average family in Tokyo spends up to 50 percent more in housing costs.

Types of Housing

In the past, traditional houses in the city were one- or two-story buildings framed with timber. Inside, the floors were covered with tatami mats. Rooms were separated by sliding doors made from a wooden frame covered by paper, which allowed the light to filter through. Today, there are still some wooden houses in Tokyo, but they have largely been replaced with high-rise apartment buildings in the central part of the city. These downtown apartments are usually very small with one or two bedrooms, a small kitchen, a living room, and a basic rest room. Some apartments do not even have showers or

◄ *Many multistory housing complexes, known as* danchi, *have been built in Tokyo and other Japanese cities to cope with the severe housing shortage.*

bathtubs; their owners use the nearest public bathhouse for washing.

Furnishings

Japanese houses and apartments tend to be simply furnished. Traditionally, rooms were used for many different purposes because of the lack of space. At night, a *futon* (mattress) would be laid on the tatami mats for sleeping. In the morning, the futon was rolled up and put away and a low table was put out for eating. Many people in Tokyo still use some traditional furnishings, but Western-style furniture is also becoming more common. It remains customary to remove your shoes when entering a home, both as a sign of respect and for reasons of cleanliness.

Another traditional practice that continues is measuring a room by the number of tatami mats it will contain. A tatami mat is usually roughly 3 feet by 6.5 feet (1 meter by 2 meters), so the size of a room will be given as a number of mats. An average house in the outer districts of Tokyo

▲ *Inside a traditional house in Tokyo, rooms are divided by sliding panels, and tatami mats cover the floor.*

Earthquake Protection

Before the technology existed to make tall structures earthquake proof, Tokyo was a city of one- or two-story buildings. During the twentieth century, new techniques designed to protect tall buildings during an earthquake were introduced, and the first skyscrapers began to appear in Tokyo. No one knows when the next "big one" will strike the city, but the earthquake that devastated Kobe in 1995, killing six thousand people, came as a grim reminder to the citizens of Tokyo that their city stands on unstable foundations.

"Of all there is to fear, that which is most fearful is earthquakes."

—Kamo no Chomei, poet.

has four or five small rooms, with a floor space of about 750 square feet (70 square meters) overall.

Family Values

Japanese parents are expected to teach their children how to behave politely and with consideration for others. Traditionally, the family has been very important in Japanese culture, with young people taught to be respectful and obedient toward older family members. Young children are pampered, not to spoil them, but so that they learn the importance of family interdependence and mutual trust. Unlike in most Western

"The nail that sticks up gets hammered down." [Meaning, individuality is not as important as loyalty to the group — so whoever stands out must learn to fit in.]

—Japanese proverb.

societies, group loyalty and consideration for others is valued more highly than independence and individuality.

School Days

Japanese children start school at the age of six. They spend six years in elementary school and another three years in junior high school. At that point, some are done with their schooling, but most go on to

▼ *All Japanese students learn English in junior high school, most often in language laboratories like this.*

further studies at senior high school and then a university or technical college. In the Metropolis of Tokyo, there are about 1,200 elementary schools, 700 junior high schools, and 400 senior high schools. In suburban areas where the population is expanding rapidly, there is often great strain on the schools' resources, but in the center of the city, where businesses have largely taken over residential areas, many schools stand empty. Like their parents, many school and college students in Tokyo commute long distances every day.

Pressure and Competition

After school, if they have any free time, Japanese children like to play with friends, watch TV, play computer games, or read comics. However, children in Japan are pushed very hard both by their teachers and by their parents. Many go to *juku* — after-class schools — in order to achieve higher grades and, in particular, to get a place at a good university.

Tokyo has over one hundred universities and colleges, but the best known is Tokyo University (known as Todai), which was founded during the Meiji period as Tokyo Imperial University. It has an excellent reputation, and most of the top politicians and other successful people in Japanese society attended it. It is said that "getting accepted almost guarantees success in life," but it is extremely difficult to get in. It is common for students to take an extra year, or even a few years, after senior high

Seijin no Hi

Seijin no Hi, or *Coming of Age Day*, is held on the second Monday in January. It marks the move into adulthood for those who turn twenty during the year. New adults dress in their best suits and kimonos, or long robes (below), and go to shrines for blessings and photos. In Tokyo, the day is celebrated at the Meiji Shrine with a traditional display of archery.

school to keep trying for the university of their choice.

▲ *Crowds of commuters fill the walkways of Shinjuku Station — Japan's busiest station — during the morning rush hour.*

Getting Around

Tokyo has one of the world's most efficient public transportation systems, a network of trains, subway trains, and buses. In the unlikely event that something goes wrong during the morning rush hour on the trains, the railroad staff hands out apology slips for workers to show their bosses. A train running a few minutes late can make headline news.

Railroad Links

Railroads link the center of Tokyo to most of the outlying suburbs, as well as other parts of Japan. The trains are fast, safe, and reliable — but they are also extremely crowded. At peak times, most trains carry many more passengers than they were designed for, and railroad companies employ people to shove commuters onto already overcrowded trains. Tokyo's main railroad station, Shinjuku, is the busiest in the world with over 2 million people passing through it every day.

Tokyo's Yamanote train line is circular, and it marks the unofficial boundary between the city's inner and outer districts. All of

Bullet Train

The shinkansen, or bullet train (left), started running in 1964, the year of the Tokyo Olympics. At first, it connected Tokyo and Osaka, but bullet trains now run to many different destinations in Japan. Although it is no longer the world's fastest train, it is still well-known for its efficiency and comfort. It is so quiet and smooth that passengers often do not realize they have left the station until they notice the scenery whizzing past the windows.

Tokyo's commuter lines and subway trains connect with it at some point. Most of the railroad lines are run by Japanese Rail, but there are also some private lines that carry commuters into the city center. Many of these lines terminate in department stores, because the store companies own and run them.

Air and Road

There are two airports serving Tokyo: Haneda International Airport and Tokyo International Airport in Narita. A monorail links the Haneda airport to the center of the city, but most international flights arrive at the newer Narita airport. Narita is 40 miles (64 km) northeast of Tokyo, outside the metropolis. The airport is linked to central Tokyo by a train service that takes about sixty minutes.

Despite huge road-building projects during the 1960s and '70s, traffic in Tokyo is very congested. Many people drive "micro" vehicles — tiny cars, vans, and trucks specially designed for the busy streets of the city. There are even garbage trucks so small that they can drive along the sidewalk. Nevertheless, because of the congestion and the difficulties and expense of parking, most commuters use public transportation.

Causes for Concern

Like many other cities, Tokyo faces a range of environmental, social, and economic problems. Some, such as congestion, pollution, overcrowding, and rising crime, are issues in cities all over the world. Others, such as the threat of earthquakes and the chaotic street system, are more specific to Tokyo. It is the city's Metropolitan Government that must deal with all these problems, trying to find long-term solutions to some difficult questions.

▲ *A pedestrian wears a linen face mask to try to avoid breathing traffic fumes in one of Tokyo's congested shopping districts.*

Tokyo's Environment

In many ways, the environment of Tokyo has improved since the 1970s, when vehicle exhaust fumes covered the city in a permanent smoky fog, or smog. New, tougher laws have improved air quality, although air pollution often still exceeds levels set by the government. Water pollution remains a problem in Tokyo's rivers and in the bay. There is also a shortage of water, as increasing amounts are needed for the ever-growing population. Tokyo draws water from reservoirs far from the city, but despite this, the city suffers regular water shortages, usually in late summer.

Another major environmental issue is garbage disposal. Every year, the city's residents throw away millions of tons of trash. Much of it goes into landfill sites that are rapidly filling up. Recent changes to the law have led to a reduction in the amount of garbage, and many residents and businesses are thinking much more carefully about recycling their trash. Perhaps surprisingly for a modern city, sanitation is another problem, as many homes are not connected to the main sewer system. However, for many residents of Tokyo, one of the most pressing problems of day-to-day life is the lack of green, open spaces, such as parks.

Social and Economic Problems

Tokyo is a cramped and busy place, and it can be a difficult city to live and work in, particularly for people with disabilities. There is also a lack of child care facilities for families where both parents wish to work, and a shortage of nursing homes for seniors. Meanwhile, many people are concerned about rising crime levels, particularly youth crime. Nevertheless, Tokyo remains a very safe city to live in.

When the booming "bubble economy" finally burst in the early 1990s, businesses in Tokyo suffered. As a result, the Metropolitan Government faced a sudden drop in tax revenue, and its income fell to crisis level, meaning that there was far less to spend on the city and its citizens. Unemployment rose rapidly, bringing with it a new sense of unease in the city. This sense of unease was heightened by a deadly subway gas attack that occurred in 1995.

The Nihonbashi Bridge

There has been a bridge across the Nihonbashi River since the beginning of the Edo period, when the bridge marked the starting point of Edo's five great highways. The present-day bridge was built in 1911 and was later topped by a highway. All distances from Tokyo to other points in Japan are measured from the Nihonbashi Bridge (above). This picture of the bridge was painted in 1840.

Governing Tokyo

Tokyo is a self-governing region, known as a prefecture. The city itself is divided into twenty-three units, known as ku (wards). The prefecture, however, also includes the Tama, a large area to the west of the city. The Tama includes twenty-six smaller cities, five towns, and eight villages. Together, the city and the Tama form the Metropolis of Tokyo.

The Metropolitan Government

The Metropolis of Tokyo has a governor, who is elected to a four-year term of office. Each ward in the city, and the cities and towns in the Tama, also have elected mayors. The powers of these local mayors are limited by laws, called ordinances, passed by the Metropolitan Government. Some services, such as the police force, are controlled centrally by the Metropolitan Government across the whole prefecture. Others, such as firefighting, water supplies, and sanitation, are run by the Metropolitan Government in the twenty-three ku only. The local governments of the cities and towns in the Tama must provide these services for their residents.

The Metropolitan Government is also in charge of nine towns and villages on the Izu and Ogasawara islands, the farthest of which lies about 600 miles (966 km) away from central Tokyo. The populations of these settlements range from 200 to 9,500 people. The most pressing priority for these far-flung regions is transportation, so the Metropolitan Government is promoting a

Gas Attack

On March 19, 1995, five members of a religious cult released sarin gas into the Tokyo subway during the morning rush hour. Sarin gas is a highly lethal nerve gas, and the attack left twelve people dead and five thousand injured. The attackers were members of a cult called Aum Shinrikyo. They have since been sentenced to death or life imprisonment.

plan to improve access by sea and by air to and from the islands.

There are 127 members of the Metropolitan Government assembly. All of these members are elected by the citizens of the prefecture every four years. The members belong to different political parties, including the Liberal Democratic Party, the Japanese Communist Party, the Komei Party, and the Democratic Party of Japan. The assembly is the decision-making body of the Metropolitan Government.

The National Government

Tokyo is also the seat of the national parliament of Japan and the Japanese prime minister, as well as being home to the emperor and the Japanese royal family. Emperor Akihito came to the throne in 1989, but he is a symbolic and ceremonial head of state with no actual political power. The Japanese Diet — the parliament — has two houses. Its members are elected. The members of the diet elect the prime minister.

▲ The two towers of the Tokyo Metropolitan Government building in Shinjuku rise above the city. The complex was designed by Japanese architect Kenzo Tange and was completed in 1991. It is the tallest building in Tokyo. The towers' patterns were inspired by the shape of windows in traditional Japanese houses.

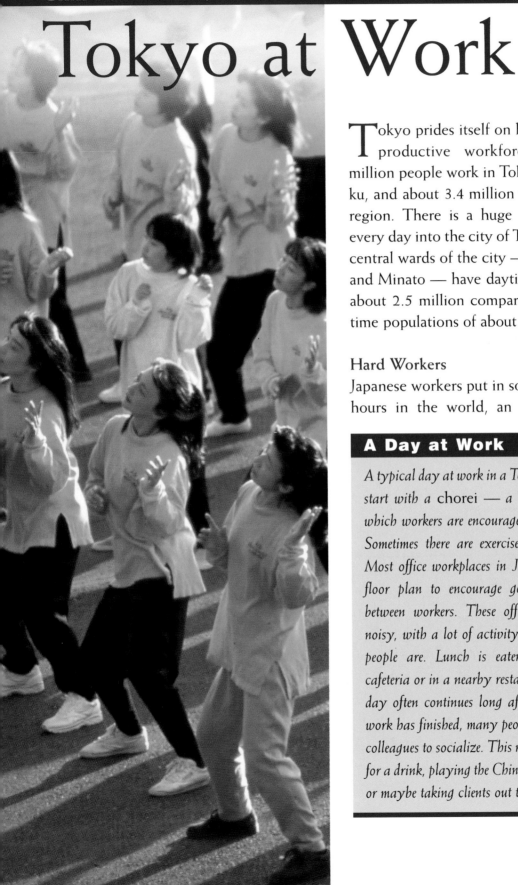

CHAPTER 4

Tokyo at Work

Tokyo prides itself on having a large and productive workforce. About 11.2 million people work in Tokyo's twenty-three ku, and about 3.4 million work in the Tama region. There is a huge influx of workers every day into the city of Tokyo; three of the central wards of the city — Chiyoda, Chuo, and Minato — have daytime populations of about 2.5 million compared to their night-time populations of about 243,000 people!

Hard Workers

Japanese workers put in some of the longest hours in the world, an average of 1,983

A Day at Work

A typical day at work in a Tokyo company may start with a chorei *— a morning meeting at which workers are encouraged to be industrious. Sometimes there are exercises and songs (left). Most office workplaces in Japan have an open floor plan to encourage good communication between workers. These offices are often very noisy, with a lot of activity to show how busy people are. Lunch is eaten in the company cafeteria or in a nearby restaurant. The working day often continues long after 5:30 P.M. After work has finished, many people go out with their colleagues to socialize. This means going to a bar for a drink, playing the Chinese game* mahjong, *or maybe taking clients out to dinner.*

> *"The driving force behind the growth of Japanese industry has been the motivation and the eagerness of industry itself..."*
>
> —Dr. Makoto Kikuchi,
> Director of the Sony Research Center.

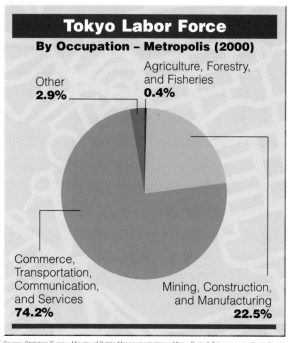

Tokyo Labor Force
By Occupation – Metropolis (2000)

Other **2.9%**

Agriculture, Forestry, and Fisheries **0.4%**

Commerce, Transportation, Communication, and Services **74.2%**

Mining, Construction, and Manufacturing **22.5%**

Source: Statistics Bureau, Ministry of Public Management, Home Affairs, Posts & Telecommunications, Japan.

hours per year (second only to workers in the United States). Most workers do many hours of unpaid overtime, and it is common for people not to take all their vacation time. This drive to work hard comes partly from a need to earn more, as housing prices and the cost of living have soared, particularly in Tokyo. It is also a result of a sense of loyalty to Japan as a country and to employers generally.

Traditional Roles

Male white-collar workers are known as *sarariman* (from the English "salaryman") in Japan. These are the workers who helped to bring about the economic success of the 1970s and 1980s. Traditionally, these men dedicated themselves to their companies and in return were assured of lifelong employment. This attitude was shaken by the economic crash of the early 1990s, but it has not entirely disappeared.

While the sarariman commuted to work, his wife traditionally stayed at home to care for the children and look after the house. For many families, this is still the case, but increasingly, women are working outside the home. Japanese husbands are unlikely to help with either the housework or the

children, so working women effectively end up with several jobs. In Tokyo, there are about 2 million female employees, most working in service industries, retail, restaurants, finance, and insurance. There are some high-powered female executives, but old attitudes still remain, and many Japanese men find the idea of a female boss difficult to cope with.

Tokyo's Industries

Tokyo is home to over 50 percent of Japan's biggest companies, including those specializing in manufacturing, finance and banking, construction, retail sales, food, entertainment, transportation, and communications. Manufacturing is an important part of Tokyo's economy. There are about 80,000 factories in Tokyo. Some

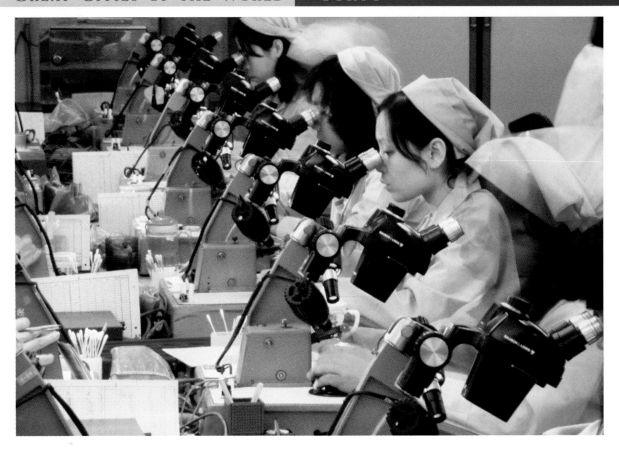

factories are huge, with between 10,000 and 20,000 employees; many others are small businesses employing as few as 20 people.

▲ *High-precision manufacturing of items such as electronic goods is important to Japan's economy.*

Newspapers and Comics

Publishing and printing is the largest industry in Tokyo, accounting for over one-fourth of all the manufacturing in the city. Most Japanese publishing companies are based in Tokyo, and most use local companies to print their material. There are more than twenty-five daily newspapers in Tokyo, all produced by newspaper companies based in the city. Between them, they have a circulation of about 25 million copies sold every day.

As well as newspapers, Japanese people love to read comic books, called *manga*. Over

2 billion manga magazines are sold in Japan every year. In fact, cartoon characters are so popular that they have a large role to play in everyday life in Japan. In Tokyo, for example, the police force is represented by a cartoon mouse, named Pi-Po chan.

Electronics

The second-largest industry in Tokyo is electronics. Japan is famous as the home of innovative products such as the Walkman, the GameBoy, and the PlayStation. Japanese companies also pioneered the use of robotics, particularly in their factories.

Japanese electronics companies such as Sony, Sanyo, Hitachi, Seiko, Mitsubishi, and Toshiba have become household names across the world.

Finance and Trade

Tokyo is the financial center for the whole of eastern Asia. During the 1980s and early 1990s, it was the fastest growing economic region in the world. The crisis of the early 1990s, when the prices of stocks and of land collapsed, left many banks and companies with huge debts. After its rapid and spectacular expansion, the economy of Japan slowed, and it has yet to recover fully. Nevertheless, Tokyo remains hugely important as a center of finance and trade, and Tokyo's business leaders are involved in many regionwide business ventures, particularly with the booming economy of China.

The Tokyo Stock Exchange is where stocks and shares are bought and sold, and it is one of the top five stock exchanges in the world, listing over 2,500 different companies and the prices of their stocks. Traditionally, the stocks and shares were bought and sold by traders who worked on the floor of the stock exchange. However, in April 1999, the hubbub of traders shouting and waving at one another was replaced with a computerized system. The trading floor is now quiet, featuring only a glass cylinder that displays prices of current stocks for onlookers.

The Tokyo Tower

Built in 1958, the Tokyo Tower (below) was modeled on Paris's Eiffel Tower, although it stands 42 feet (13 m) taller than the Eiffel Tower, at 1,100 feet (335 m). At the time of its construction, it dominated Tokyo's skyline, but although it remains Tokyo's highest vantage point, it has since been joined by numerous skyscrapers. It is a transmitting tower for both radio and television, but it is also a huge tourist attraction, with a waxwork museum, an aquarium, and other amusements — as well as a spectacular view from the top!

CHAPTER 5

Tokyo at Play

In their spare time, the residents of Tokyo enjoy the theater, movies, or trips to one of the city's amazing entertainment complexes, which feature movie theaters, stores, bars, bowling alleys, and play areas under one roof. They also like going to restaurants and coffee bars or shopping in the city's glamorous malls. At night, whole districts of the city come alive with people visiting bars and nightclubs. Tokyo is truly a vibrant, twenty-four-hour city, offering a wide choice of entertainment.

Traditional Entertainment and Culture

Many people like to watch performances of the traditional theater forms of *noh*, bunraku, and kabuki. There are also many small museums and craft studios in Sumida where people can admire and learn traditional art forms such as pottery, doll- and mask-

"The cherry-blossoms
In the precincts of the shrine
Are Spring's offering to the Deity.
Many a place is famed for cherry-trees,
But none can boast such blossoms;..."

—Excerpt from *Tamura Noh* drama.

◀ *A performance of a* noh *play. Noh is the oldest of the three traditional forms of Japanese drama, dating back to the fourteenth century.*

making, and calligraphy (handwriting). As the capital of Japan, Tokyo is also a cultural center, with many museums and art galleries.

▲ *The Kabuki-za Theater is the place in Tokyo to see kabuki. Performances can last up to five hours.*

Theater

Noh drama is an ancient mixture of dance, recitation, and music. In Tokyo, it can be seen at the National Noh Theater in Shibuya. Bunraku is drama acted out by three large puppets, which are usually operated by three puppeteers. As the puppets move onstage, the story is recited by a group of offstage readers. Bunraku is staged in Tokyo at the National Theater in Chiyoda. Kabuki features gorgeous costumes, colorful sets, and exaggerated gestures and makeup to tell melodramatic stories. Performances can last many hours. The main venue for performances of kabuki in Tokyo is the

Kabuki-za Theater in Ginza. It opened in 1889 but was rebuilt twice during the twentieth century. It is designed for kabuki, with a revolving stage and a raised runway that projects into the audience area.

Ueno

Tokyo's Ueno district is home to Ueno Park, where people walk during springtime to admire the cherry blossoms. The park also contains some of Tokyo's major museums, including the Tokyo National Museum, the National Museum of Western Art, the Tokyo Metropolitan Museum of Art, and the National Science Museum. The Tokyo National Museum contains more than 89,000 artifacts illustrating all aspects of Japan's long history. A building designed by the great architect Le Corbusier houses the National Museum of Western Art, with a collection that includes many paintings by the French Impressionist painters. The Tokyo Metropolitan Museum of Art is mostly underground and showcases modern Japanese art. The National Science Museum is immediately recognizable by the lifesize model of a blue whale outside its main entrance.

▼ *Tokyo is a good place for buying the latest in electronics. There are hundreds of electronics shops in the Akihabara area, known as "Electric Town."*

Tosho-gu Shrine

The Tosho-gu Shrine, in Ueno Park, is one of the few seventeenth-century (early Edo) structures in Tokyo to survive both earthquakes and World War II bombs. The shrine was established in 1627, and the buildings date from 1651. The shrine is dedicated to the first Tokugawa shogun, Ieyasu. The path from the stone entry arch to the shrine itself is lined with two hundred stone lanterns, called ishidoro, which were given as gifts by the daimyo (landholding lords) in the Edo period.

Shopping

Fashion is an obsession with many Tokyo residents. Expensive Western designer labels such as Hermes, Prada, and Gucci continue to sell well despite the recession of the 1990s. Japanese designers such as Issey Miyake and Comme des Garçons are also very popular. The major shopping areas are in Ikebukuro, Shibuya, and Shinjuku, all of which have large department stores and shopping plazas. Other areas have smaller stores — for example, fashion boutiques in Harajuku and Aoyama, bookstores in Jimbocho, and stores selling electronic products in Akihabara.

Popular Spots

For a day out in the city, many Tokyo residents head for Odaiba (Rainbow Town). This whole district has been built on land reclaimed from the sea in Tokyo Bay and is a favorite destination for many residents. Attractions include the Toyota MegaWeb, which is the largest car showroom in Japan; one of the world's biggest Ferris wheels, 380 feet (116 m) high, at Pallette Town; and a large artificial beach. There is also some extraordinary architecture, notably the Fuji Television Building, which has a huge ball on its roof.

Nightlife

The Japanese rarely entertain in their homes — probably because of lack of space — so dining out and having fun in the evening is big business in Tokyo. Some bars have

▼ *Playing* pachinko *in one of Tokyo's large amusement halls is very popular. Pachinko, which is somewhat like pinball, involves flicking metal balls into winning holes on the screen.*

Vending Machines

It is possible to buy almost anything out of a vending machine in Tokyo. These machines are on almost every street corner in the city. As well as beverages and cigarettes, vending machines sell batteries, ties, tights, flower arrangements, videos, magazines, phone cards, hot noodles, and rice. Anyone trying to vandalize a machine is immediately caught on a digital camera, and a sensor sets off an alarm at the nearest police station.

karaoke machines. These machines play an instrumental background, allowing customers to come forward and sing along with their favorite song. However, most karaoke now takes place without an audience in specially built "boxes" (small rooms). Another favorite pastime is *pachinko*,

a type of pinball machine. For those who want to dance the night away, Tokyo's clubs and discos stay open all night, and some are open well into the next day. The best-known clubs and discos are found in the Shinjuku and Roppongi districts.

Sports

Traditional Japanese sports such as *sumo* and the martial arts are very popular in Japan. Sumo wrestling is Japan's national sport. Its history dates back two thousand years, and it combines Shinto rituals with athleticism and agility. The rules are quite simple — the loser of a sumo match is the first to step out of the ring or to touch the ground with any part of his body except his feet. The referee oversees the match and declares the winner. Sumo tournaments take place in Tokyo three times a year at the Kokugikan Stadium.

Baseball, soccer, and golf are the main "Western" sports in Japan. Tokyo has three baseball teams — the Yomiuri Giants, the Nippon Ham Fighters, and the Yakult Swallows. The first two teams have their home at the Tokyo Dome; the Yakult Swallows are based out of the Jingu Baseball Stadium. Most games are held in the evening to a backdrop of incredible noise from the teams' supporters. Soccer is not as popular as baseball, but it received a boost in 2002 when the World Cup Finals were

◄ *Sumo wrestlers line up for the opening ceremony of a tournament at the Kokugikan sumo hall in Tokyo.*

"A wise man climbs Fuji once;
only a fool climbs it twice."

—Japanese proverb.

held in Japan and South Korea. Golf is an expensive hobby in Tokyo. There are nineteen golf courses in the city, but only three of these are public, and the fees for membership in private clubs are huge. Driving ranges across the city give eager golfers a chance to practice their shots.

Outdoor Pursuits

For those who want to escape the city, there are many destinations in the regions surrounding the city that can be reached easily by train. Hakone is a 1.5-hour ride from the Shinjuku station, and it provides a welcome breath of fresh air for millions of Tokyo residents every year. The region is mountainous, with beautiful scenery and many hot springs. The temple town of Kamakura is about an hour's train journey away. It was the capital of Japan during the Kamakura period (1185-1333), and it has many temples and shrines dating from that time. Another popular day trip from Tokyo is to Nikko. This has been a sacred Buddhist site since the eighth century. It is also home to the mausoleum of Tokugawa Ieyasu and has many other shrines and temples as well.

► *The Great Buddha at the Kotokuin Temple in*
Kamakura was created in 1252.

Climbing Mount Fuji

Many Japanese people hope to climb Mount Fuji once in their lifetime. In fact, about 2 million people climb the 12,388-foot (3,776-m) volcano every year. The main climbing season is July and August, as Fuji is covered with snow for the rest of the year. People try to reach the summit in time for goraiko — sunrise. Mount Fuji last erupted in 1707, so it is officially a dormant volcano. Nevertheless, the people in the town of Fujiyoshida, which stands at the foot of the mountain, offer prayers every August to the Fire God to prevent a new eruption.

Looking Forward

Tokyo is at a turning point in its history. The city looks as if it is rich, glamorous and thriving — and in international terms, it is. Japan is the third largest economy after the United States and China. Technologically, Japan is still the second most powerful economy (after the United States), and it remains the world leader in robotics. Tokyo still attracts businesses and tourists. Yet government plans to set the national economy of Japan back on track after the recession of the 1990s have not been effective, and the Tokyo Metropolitan Government has huge debts. The city also has problems with pollution and transportation, and crime is rising.

The National Capital Relocation Plan

Conditions in Tokyo's downtown have become so difficult that the Japanese national parliament has proposed that many of Tokyo's functions as the capital city be moved to other parts of Japan. In 1999, the parliament published a report giving details of suggested new locations for the parliament and various other government organizations. Not surprisingly, the Tokyo Metropolitan Government has responded with outrage. In 1990, in its reply to the parliament's report, the Tokyo Metropolitan Government agreed

◀ *This is typical Tokyo — neon signs, lines of traffic, and crowds of people on a busy street in Ginza.*

The John Lennon Museum

About forty minutes from central Tokyo by train, in the Saitama Super Arena, the John Lennon Museum is probably the only museum in the world devoted to a single rock musician. With the full approval of John Lennon's widow, Yoko Ono, it opened on October 9, 2000, the day that would have been Lennon's sixtieth birthday. The museum attracts local people and tourists alike. They walk through nine zones that mark the stages of John Lennon's life, from early childhood onward. Even the restaurant is a copy of John's favorite eating place, with some of his favorite meals on the menu.

that when the parliament passed the resolution to relocate, there were many growing problems in Tokyo, such as traffic congestion and housing shortages. The reply claims, however, that since that time, many changes have taken place that now make the relocation plan unnecessary.

Twenty-first Century Tokyo

The Tokyo Metropolitan Government has come up with plans to improve living, traveling, and working conditions in the whole prefecture. In 1997, the city launched "Plans for the Creation of a Resident-Friendly Tokyo." This was followed by the "Tokyo Plan 2000." The plan covers the next fifteen years but looks ahead for fifty years, and it has sixteen policy goals ranging from

"A global city that attracts a large number of visitors."

—Basic vision of the Tokyo Plan 2000.

creating "an urban environment that facilitates a balance between work and home life" to increasing "the appeal of Tokyo to make it an unrivaled world city." As usual, Tokyo is planning and thinking big!

▼ *The Tokyo Plan 2000 offers guidelines to Tokyo's citizens, businesses, and local governments, inviting them to help build a prosperous future for the city. The plan also aims to ensure that Tokyo remains the political, economic, and cultural heart of Japan.*

Time Line

1457 Ota Dokan begins to build Edo Castle and the town of Edo is founded.

1590 Tokugawa Ieyasu takes control of the region around Edo.

1603 Ieyasu becomes shogun and makes Edo the center of government.

1639 The Tokugawa shoguns close Japan off from the outside world.

1657 The Meireki Fire rages for three days and destroys large parts of Edo.

1707 Mount Fuji erupts, covering Edo in ash.

1750 Edo has over 1 million inhabitants.

1853 The United States sends a fleet of warships to open diplomatic and trade links with Japan.

1868 The Japanese imperial family moves from Kyoto to Edo. City is renamed "Tokyo." The Meiji period begins.

1888 The first Imperial Palace is built on the grounds of Edo Castle in Tokyo.

1912 The Meiji period ends.

1914 Tokyo Station opens.

1923 The Great Kanto earthquake and subsequent fires destroy much of Tokyo.

1927 The first subway line opens between Asakusa and Ueno.

1931 The Haneda International Airport in Tokyo is completed.

1941 The Port of Tokyo opens. Japan attacks Pearl Harbor and enters World War II.

1945 Tokyo suffers devastating bombing, which kills or injures many thousands of Tokyo residents. World War II ends.

1949 Tokyo is organized into 23 ku (wards).

1958 The Tokyo Tower is completed.

1964 The Olympic Games are held in Tokyo. First bullet train runs between Tokyo and Osaka.

1968 The Imperial Palace, which was destroyed during the bombings of World War II, is rebuilt.

1973 Oil crisis briefly affects Japanese economy.

1989 Emperor Akihito comes to the throne.

Early 1990s The so-called "bubble economy" comes to an end.

1991 The Metropolitan Government building opens in Shinjuku.

1995 The Aum Shinrikyo release sarin gas on a Tokyo subway train, killing twelve.

2002 The World Cup Finals are held in Japan and South Korea.

Glossary

bento a traditional lunchbox, containing cold rice, vegetables, a little meat or fish, pickles, and a slice of fruit.

bubble economy when the prices of property, stocks, and shares rise very quickly, to be eventually followed by a sudden drop in prices.

Buddhism religion that follows the teachings of "the Buddha" (the "Enlightened One"), seeking peace and an end to suffering through living a pure and simple life.

bunraku classical puppet theater, using almost life-size puppets operated by three puppeteers who are visible on stage. As the puppets move, the story is recited by a group of offstage readers.

burakumin a social group of Japanese people that suffers discrimination because their ancestors did jobs once considered "unclean," such as slaughtering animals, butchering, or leather work. In the past, burakumin were forced to live together in settlements apart from the rest of society.

commuter someone who travels to work in the city from a home that is in the suburbs or an outlying area.

conurbation mass of towns.

daimyo landholding warrior lords in the time of the shoguns.

Diet the Japanese parliament.

dynasty series of rulers from the same family.

Edo original name for Tokyo before 1868 and the Meiji period.

expatriate someone who lives abroad.

geisha a refined and elegant woman who is an expert in the arts and entertaining guests.

kabuki traditional Japanese theater with lavish costumes, in which all the roles are acted by men.

kami Shinto gods or spirits associated with natural objects such as mountains and springs.

karaoke popular entertainment in which people sing along to taped music without the vocal track.

konketsu people of mixed ancestry.

ku city ward, an administrative area that is part of the Tokyo prefecture.

Kyoto old royal city, seat of the imperial family until 1868.

noh ancient Japanese drama, performed on a bare stage with masked actors.

pachinko pinball machine game that is hugely popular in Japan.

prefecture one of the self-governing regions into which Japan is divided.

samurai a member of the Japanese warrior class in the time of the shoguns.

sarariman (salaryman) a male employee of a large company.

sashimi thinly sliced raw fish.

shinkansen the bullet train, Japan's high-speed train.

Shintoism ancient Japanese religion that honors spirits in all living things and natural forms, such as mountains, rivers, and rocks.

shitamachi traditionally in Edo, the low-lying area outside the castle walls where the ordinary people lived, centered in Ueno and in Asakusa.

shogun the military ruler of Japan before the Meiji Restoration in 1868.

sumo Japan's national sport, combining Shinto ritual with agile wrestling.

tatami floor mats made from straw and covered with a smooth layer of rush (a grasslike plant). Outdoor shoes should never be worn on tatami mats.

yamanote traditionally in Edo, the high-level ground in and around the castle.

Further Information

Books

Edwards, Betty. *Tokyo Friends: Tokyo No Tomodachi*. Charles E. Tuttle, 1999.

Hall, Eleanor J. *Life Among the Samurai (The Way People Live)*. Lucent Books, 1998.

Kallen, Stuart A. *Life in Tokyo (The Way People Live)*. Lucent Books, 2001.

Kaoru, Ono. *Sushi for Kids*. Charles E. Tuttle, 2003.

Kato, Kumi. *Watashi No Nihon Book III: My Day in Tokyo* (Vol.3). Charles E. Tuttle, 1995.

Kent, Deborah. *Tokyo (Cities of the World)*. Scholastic Library, 1997.

Web Sites

www.tnm.go.jp/scripts/index.en.idc
The Tokyo National Museum web site with exhibits and information.

www.chijihonbu.metro.tokyo.jp/english/
The Tokyo Metropolitan Government web site.

www.jsf.or.jp/index_e.html
The Tokyo National Science Museum web site.

www.travelforkids.com/Funtodo/Japan/tokyo.htm
Travel for Kids with information on interesting places to visit in Tokyo.

www.factmonster.com/ce6/world/A0848968.html
Fact Monster information on the history, economy, and landmarks of Tokyo.

www.mid-tokyo.com/18_e/aboutthis.html
Mid-Tokyo Maps with moving, interactive maps of Tokyo during the Edo period and today.

Index